Edited by K.A. Dutton
Cover Design www.canva.com

This book is a work of fiction. Names, characters, places, and incidents either are products of the author's imagination or are used fictitiously. Any resemblance to actual persons, living or dead, events, or locales is entirely coincidental.

ISBN: 9781980465355

To the writers that made this book a scary reality.

CONTENTS

The School 1
The Lake 13
The Room 27
The Asylum 39
The Basement 55
The Road 65
Christmas Dinner 75
The Ship 93
Author Biographies 101
Acknowledgements 103

THE SCHOOL

By K.A. Dutton

"It's freezing!" Jordan's teeth chattered as his hands grasped the frozen metal gate. He yanked himself over the top with haste and tucked his hands under his pits. Instantly regretting his decision to leave his gloves at home.

Frost glazed the fields of grass. The autumn leaves were long fallen and rotten. But a few clung on and whistled through the late-night breeze. An owl frozen with determination, focussed its eyes on any potential food. It ignored the group of teenagers, waiting for juicy mice to scuttle out of hiding.

Jordan, Andrew, Stewart, and Riley, made their way up the paved hill. Their school loomed in the distance, misted in the fog that threatened to consume it. They weren't afraid of it. They rejoiced and bragged. *Oh*, how rebellious they were for breaking into school. The image of their parents' reactions tickled them, they revelled the thought.

A stone archway greeted them. It towered menacingly over their figures, its moonlit shadow alone intimidated them to the bone. Within each crack of the brick work, with each vine that grew and made home, this archway stood proudly.

"Guys, maybe we shouldn't..." said Riley. She shivered under her parka coat. Strands of hair fell loosely across her face, a failed attempt at stuffing it all under the knitted beanie hat. Her nose was bright red from the cold, and all she could think about was how she would much rather be at home.

Andrew scoffed, and pulled at the strings on her parka. "Don't be such a girl."

"-Bite me!" Riley barked back. The anger from Andrews statement bubbled inside her, it sent a surge of fire to every bone, muscles tensed ready to attack.

"Cut it out," said Stewart. "We are on a mission."

Inside the Old Hall, Helga Davenport sensed the disturbance. But, how couldn't she? Every word, whisper, syllable, echoed in this vast building.

The off-white linen garnet shift dress she would wear to bed, was now ashen and diluted by time. But she still enjoyed twirling around, her skirt flew without the confinement of gravity. Each twirl would let out a breeze of her own. It would make the stained-glass windows shudder.

"What was that?!" Cried Jordan, making Riley jump.

"Just the wind, jeez Jordan." Even though Andrew panicked for a moment there too, he didn't recall feeling the breath of wind. The light air wasn't enough to shake the windows of the school; it was probably just a small gust.

Helga sighed as she drifted absently form room to room.

"Aunt Helen slept there." She groaned.

Next room,

"Brother Elliot *loved* it in here." She rolled her eyes.

And the next room, she paused.

She knew from all her years that the carpet had been changed 26 times, the walls painted 14 before being covered in patterned paper. And shelves were drilled into the walls her that father had crafted with his sweat and blood.

She tossed the book off the shelf without even touching it, not like she could anyway. "Books are so boring," she remarked as it hit the ground with a thump.

Finally, the room where her father would play beautiful music. It would echo off the glistening walls, the soft light reflected in her Mothers' gentle eyes.

It was now a classroom. Littered with chairs, tables, stains strewn across the vintage carpet.

Helga used to be bothered by it all. It hurt when they took all her belongings, when the pictures of her were taken down. But it hurt the most waiting for someone to join her.

It's not often Helga is disturbed during her nightly walks. She hears the howls of laughter- children's laughter. A phantom of her younger self. Hair in pig tails. Dancing around, plucking flowers. Laughing at nothing. But laughing turned to mocking as she smirks at the version of herself trapped in time.

Watching the children from the stained-glass window on the 2nd floor. Her gaze is drawn to her own faded reflection. A frozen phantom of what once was.

The hair she so longed to run her fingers through. To feel the sensation of her Mother brushing it with a wire brush, tugging at the knots and tearing the follicles from her scalp. An experience she took for granted at the time.

Now, watching a young girl in man's clothes. *How ghastly.*

Even in the colder months, Helga adored her dresses. Her father would bring her a new one, every time he returned from his long journeys. Dresses were her favourite possessions. She couldn't watch as they took them away, her mother clawing at them with tears streaming down her blushing cheeks. Clawing so desperately at the last fragments that proved Helga's short existence on his earth.

Jordan lead the group to the main hall. Lighting the sweetly scented candles stolen from the bathroom back home. There was a persistent whistle in the hall, it made all the strands of hair stand up on each of the children.

Placing themselves in a circle, with the candles dimly lit around them. Andrew pulled out a torch, beating it against the palm of his hand until it sprung to life.

"Who wants to start?" Stewart asked.

Riley, her eyes darted around the hall. She squinted at the dark corners, afraid there's a figure lurking. "I don't like it here, why didn't we pick our form room?"

Andrew rolled his eyes, "Stop being such a baby. I'll start."

Riley took a breath, her eyebrows knitted together.

"So there once was-"

"-I swear if this is about the Robertson twins-"

"It's not, shut up." Andrew barked, "Right."

"So, there's always been rumours of ghosts in the school. Circling the halls, slamming doors shut. And that if you are still wandering around when class is in session, you'll most likely see one. But those are all lies."

Stewart, puzzled. "I thought this was meant to be a scary story?"

"It is," Andrew said. "But this is a story of the real ghost. The true one. Not one in the rumours.

This is the story of Helga and how her family *mysteriously* died."

Helga had lost sight of the children. Then she noticed it; small flickers of light that would have been invisible to the human eye, was clear to her.

If she could taste, or even salivate. She would savour the essence of her blood as her teeth penetrated her bottom lip. The metallic notes, and surge of deviance, would taste divine.

"Helga- Helga Davenport? Like Mrs Davenport, our English teacher?" croaked Riley.

Andrew sighed, "No. Not like Mrs Davenport. But it is ironic they share the surname. It was Helga's Dad that built this place, ya know."

"As I was saying. Helga had a huge family, at least 5 brothers. She was the only girl though. The second youngest was sick with the plague... or so they thought."

Riley listened intently.

"So, on a long winter night. Much like this one. He died. But Mr Davenport was suspicious. They soon discovered it wasn't the plague that killed their son."

Stewart was highly skeptical, "Why would they even bother checking? The plague could have killed them all. Surely disposing of the infected body was a priority, not a dumb autopsy. Did they even have autopsies in those days?"

"Shush," growled Riley.

Stewart fell silent.

Andrew continued, "They suspected it was the eldest. Who found out he wouldn't be inheriting the fortune or the manor when their parents inevitably die."

"This suspicion was even more concrete when another sibling fell sick. The second eldest- Elliot. When the doctor arrived, he wasn't entirely convinced it was the plague. But the symptoms were the same as the other brother."

"However. When the eldest son died after Elliot's passing, it was a mystery. The Doctors were adamant it wasn't the plague, but something was killing them. With Helga and two brothers left, Mr and Mrs

Davenport were determined to find the cause before their whole family met their untimely end."

Helga found it amusing. How did these children know so much? It was the first time she heard her story from another perspective. But they treated it like an old wife's tale.

She remembered Sam's last words. The eldest.

He whispered only to her in his last moments.

"*Don't go near Mother.*"

All the children jumped out of their skin when a door slammed open. A gust of wind raised goose bumps on their arms and sent shivers down their spines. But no one entered. And when they tried to enter through that door earlier, they were positively certain it was air tight shut.

When Jordan stood up, he limped over as his legs tingled with pins and needles. Closing the door after looking both ways outside, there wasn't a being in sight. "It's nothing guys. The wind must have broken the lock. The door is like a hundred years old, at least." But he said it more to reassure himself, than to put the others at ease. "Go on, Andrew."

"Right." Andrew breathed. Slowing down his heart after that surprise. "The eyes of the town turned to the parents. No one else held grudges, or any motives, to be targeting the family. Mr Davenport was arrested and held at the station. Before he too, died 3 days later after displaying plague-like symptoms. He died in the hospital, separated from his family."

"Mrs Davenport was broken. She was hopeless, and helpless, and was crossed off as a suspect as they couldn't arrest the only surviving parent of the three Davenport children that remained.

But she didn't give up. They searched, pondered, and researched all about what disease or poison was ailing the family. When the murderer slipped. The gardener found a mushroom."

Helga recalled the very day.

"This is no mushroom I have ever seen before, Ma'am." The gardener said to her Mother.

Her Mother, Jane Davenport, raised the mushroom against the falling sun. "Get this to the doctor immediately. And search for where these could be growing."

Jane pinched Helga's cheeks. "Don't worry, darling. I won't let anything happen to you."

"The mushrooms were growing in the nearby forest. Protected and hidden under a fallen Oak. And the mushroom was called- The Deadly Webcap.

The Doctor explained that it shared similar symptoms to that of the plague. Whilst the boy's death could have been explained as one of their adventures, as they usually do to occupy their time, they could have easily eaten the mushrooms accidentally. But Mrs Davenport was certain that Mr Davenport would have recognised the mushroom immediately. Since it was the very mushroom that killed both his parents when he was younger."

"Wait, wait, wait. When did this become a mystery? Aren't we here to tell scary stories?"

"Fine. I'll rush it." Andrew stood proudly. Grabbing the torch light and holding it under his chin to illuminate his glaring eyes. "It was Helga!" he exclaimed. "It's said that when the cook wasn't looking. Helga slipped in the mushrooms with her family's dinner. She would help carry out the plates, much to the family's amusement as they watched her balance the food and shake under the weight of it."

Riley cried. "But why would she kill her own family?"

Andrew raised his shoulders. "No clue."

"Wait, that's it?" asked Jordan. Crossing his arms with difficulty through the thickness of his coat. "You can't end the story there."

Andrew brushed back his ash blonde hair back after turning off the torch. "Okay. I don't know how she died. But legend has it she still lurks around the school today. Apparently, she had a whole box of them stashed under her bed, and they sent her to an institution as soon as they found out. Few years later, the rest of her siblings passed away due to natural causes and her mother begged for them to let her return home."

Helga couldn't help the grin on her face. She was legendary.

But the truth is, she didn't know why she did it. She was simply bored with too many brothers that wouldn't play with her. Her father left home too often, and there's only so much tolerance for her Mother.

After spending 10 years in that ghastly institute, she was brought home. She would rather the institute, so she took a handful of the mushrooms and ate them like chocolate. Laughing in her Mother's face as she was going to be left alone, in this unnecessarily large mansion as a permanent reminder that everyone she had ever loved was dead, until death took her too.

But Helga was hungry.

Riley stood up and stomped her foot. The heel of her shoe sounding an echo. "Ugh. I've had enough. You just wasted our time for nothing. I'm going home."

Stewart uttered the final words, "wait!" to catch Riley's attention. Before all the children were in the presence of Helga's ghostly figure. Her eyes wild and hungry, as the hall echoed with screams.

Then silence, much to Helga's preference.

THE LAKE

By Lily Noova

My father loved Africa. He loved the freedom of exploration that his travels granted him. I was always so excited to hear him coming home after so many months away, and I would listen intently to his fascinating stories. On the other hand, Mother wasn't too pleased. She was afraid that one of his adventures would get him killed one day, and she was right.

I was ten when my father traveled to Kenya searching for some artifacts near Ol Doinyo Lengai, *Mountain of God* in the Maasai language. The reports said that he drowned in a nearby lake, but they couldn't retrieve the body. Shortly after the news, we received a box of his belongings that were gathered by the friends he was camping with. Mother didn't let me open this box, she stuffed it in the furthest corner of the attic, until she passed on shortly after my 25th birthday.

The box was just lost memories. How was I supposed to remember something from 15 years ago? I cleared the attic out with my sister and we both took a moment. We sat beside the box, ignoring the layers of dust around us, and held each other. Mother didn't want us to open it for a reason.

Annie brushed the dust off, revealing our family name drawn on in felt tip.

"We should open it," she said.

When you lose a parent young, you have this picture of them in your head. Some memories were real, some are distorted, and some are ones you made up. I was scared that opening this box would mean that picture would change. To me, my father was this great adventurer, fearless, and strong. But that picture could be fictional, and this box was real.

I turned to her, a lump forming in my throat, choking the words out. "Okay."

The lid of the box was stiff with age, but the contents stood the test of time. Packed neatly together were a few of his History and Geography books, along with a few torches with dead batteries.

Then I found something I never thought I would see again. It was the journal that my father used and the one that he would read from when he told us his exciting stories.

I clutched it in my hands, my fingers itching to open it.

Annie sobbed and with a nod of her agreement, we opened the book to the last entry.

October 23rd, 1995. Kenya.

* * *

"Phillip Morris." A round-faced short man shook the hand of his new companion. The explorer usually traveled alone. "I look for lost, buried, destroyed or forgotten artefacts. Hope it's fine if I join your camp for a while. I carelessly forgot about charging any of my electronic supplies."

"Feel at home", the companion answered and invited the Phillip with a hand wave gesture. His skin was pale despite the fact he wore little to no protection from the harsh African sun and his chest hair poked out of his tight shirt with the buttons ready to pop at any given second. He gave Phillip a wide smile, that reassured his mind that he could trust this man. "We have enough electricity in here."

"*Kenya.*" Phillip chuckled, and the man nodded knowingly.

Phillip strutted to the free spot and put his backpack down. He had not expected to see a group of this size in the area and it was a real blessing for his situation. He did not know why, but this time his expedition had not gone well from the very beginning: first he had missed his flight and now his batteries refused to work, and he had no working lights. More importantly, he had not taken any spare supplies with him. He was usually very organized, but this time...

He got his journal out of the backpack and scribbled the date: "Oct 23rd, 1995". That's a start. Writing in his tent until fatigue got the better of him.

But it wasn't soon until a strange sound awoke him up and Phillip grabbed his flashlight without hesitation. He pressed the knob several times, but it did not help a bit. The man swore and threw the flashlight aside, getting out of his self-made refuge. It was impossible to see anything in this thick darkness; the moon barely illuminated the silhouettes of the tents. Phillip saw a lonely lantern swinging on a stick near the campfire and headed towards it.

The sound repeated itself, which made Phillip pause and instantly regret getting out of his tent. He was motionless for a few moments with his eyes set on the lantern as if it were the only dry spot on a sinking island. He grabbed it and squeezed the handle slowly turning back. But there was nobody around.

Now that the mild light of the lantern was helping Phillip to see, he carefully and slowly followed the windings of the road. He stepped at the very edge of the cliff, where the road wound and ran down to the jungle and looked back around. Not sure how to feel about the sounds he had just heard, Phillip turned back to the camp when the cry repeated itself. This frightening sound came from the jungle.

Phillip froze, too frightened to turn back. His heart started beating faster and sweat trickled down his forehead. It was smart to wake the people in the camp up and ask them to look around. They were a bunch of trained folks with the necessary equipment and nerves of steel, that was for sure. Phillip could say that judging by their leader he had met earlier this morning. But he did not want to look weak or pathetic either.

What if it was just the sound of the local birds or some unknown animals? Waking up the campers would be a bad choice in this case. He needed to be sure that there was a real danger in front of him. The man shook his head and faced the jungle. He would give the place a quick look, and if it was something awful, he would rush toward the camp immediately and ask for the help. This plan looked reasonable.

Keeping the lantern high and next to his face, Phillip slowly went down into the jungle and entered the sacred place; however, the trees did not stick around for too long. Just a few steps behind him, the man managed to see some silhouettes walking and moving. The light of the lantern revealed some shades falling from the objects in front of him. He continued to walk, scared as much to turn back and run as to further his adventure. Phillip exited the jungle and froze for a moment, trying to grasp what he was left with.

The huge lake the man was looking at was not beautiful or captivating but had an unexplainable allure of the dead place. The air around was special, and the surface was so attractive in its stillness that Phillip could not resist staring at it. But it was not the lake a normal person would expect to see. The water was still and grey, with no movement of waves that would indicate any life in there. It was a dead lake with no movements. However...

Phillip looked closely and noticed the silhouette of a bird sitting still in the middle of the lake. The man was surprised by such a picture. The lake did not seem alive to him, and this bird was not moving either. Holding his breath, the traveler came closer and sat on the shore. He stretched his arm out and lifted the lantern to observe the surface. He could now make out that the water was red.

“Blood...?” Phillip whispered and wanted to touch the water, but the same sound he had already heard earlier stunned him and made him drop the lantern in the lake. The man tried to catch the lamp, but it went out immediately and became as hard a stone being stuck on the surface as if preparing to be reborn as a new creature. Phillip fell on his rear and crawled back to the jungle. At this very moment, the bird, which was staying still in the middle of the lake, raised and stretched its wings preparing to fly. Frozen by what he was seeing, the man was scared to breathe and merely watched what was happening. The bird arose and cried.

The sound spread all over the jungle, making leaves tremble.

While this creature was floating on the lake, other small and big birds and animals started to come to the surface, moaning and crying, crawling toward the only visitor they had today. One of the flamingoes appeared almost at the shore.

The half-rotted body of the bird slowly moved toward Phillip, staring at him with the sparkling but empty holes in its skull. The man could see the bones and the decomposing flesh dangling off. The bird’s legs did not have any skin on them, and he could see the movement of their cartilages as it strode.

"Help me...", the bird croaked vibrating with her chest. A few feathers fell as it spoke. "I want to live."

Petrified, the man closed his eyes, trying not to look at the corpse of the bird coming to life and talking to him. However, it did not help much. He could hear their cries and moans and feel them coming closer.

"I want to live..."

Phillip could not bear this anymore. Having jumped on his feet, he rushed back to the camp. He hoped that these creatures would not follow him through the jungle, but he was too scared to look back and make sure. He ran, slipping and stumbling and stopped only when he reached the hill. The man fell on his knees and elbows, breathing heavily.

Eventually, he looked back. Nobody was pursuing him.

He sat on the hill and came back to breathing normally. The first thing he wanted to do was rush to the camp and tell others what he saw. But... Who would believe him? Those brave men would only laugh at him. At this moment, the man was even almost sad that none of the creatures were following him. This way he would not have to explain anything. He sat on the hill for a while, waiting for something to happen, but in vain. No more sound followed and none of the creatures came out of the jungle.

Spotting the sunrise, Phillip slowly dragged himself to the tent he was sleeping in. He decided to ask the campers about the place tomorrow morning. Maybe they could even come with him the next day and see it in the daylight. With this spare time, he scribbled what had happened in his journal.

Phillip got out of his lair when all the camp was already awake. He stopped next to the tent and put the hand on his forehead to cover his face from the sun.

"Did not know that you, explorers, love sleeping that long", he heard a familiar voice right next to him and turned back.

"Hi, sir", he answered. "Was quite a night."

"Nightmares?" The tall man smiled and put his arms to his side. "We are going to the top of Ol Doinyo Lengai. Care to join us?"

"Ol Doniyo... what?", Phillip asked. The man chuckled.

"Mountain of God, if you wish. I'll tell you more on the go."

"Is it possible to see the lake here... From the top?", Phillip inquired, following the man from the camp.

"Lake Natron? South of here?" His companion was surprised "Yes. Why?"

"Is it a special lake or something?"

"It depends what you call special, Mr. Morris."

"Please. Phillip."

"Sure, Phillip", the man nodded. "Why are you asking?"

"I think I might have seen something." Phillip lowered his voice and whispered: "Creatures and animals from the lake."

His guide stopped and they let others from the camp go ahead.

"Anything wrong, sir?" One of the campers asked, seeing the interruption. "Should we stop?"

"Move on!" Answered the tall man immediately. "We will cover your back"

When everyone passed, they continued to walk, but this time silently for a moment.

"What did you see exactly, Phillip?" He asked.

"I told you. Creatures. From the lake."

"Birds? Animals?"

"How did you...?" Phillip was shocked, but his companion stopped him.

"There is a legend. About the lake." He smiled "I was hoping that somebody one day would confirm that, but it never happened to anyone I know of."

"What legend?" Phillip gulped.

"According to Maasai, this is a dead lake. It has red colour, the colour of blood, and it is thought to be cursed by the gods. It is the only lake that takes lives away instead of giving them. The person who sees the creatures of the lake..." The man stopped and fell silent abruptly.

"What?" The traveler could feel shivers going down his spine, "The person who sees the creatures of the lake what?"

"Is cursed", the man answered and looked right into Phillip's eyes. "Have you been in a place where you did something disgraceful? Did you rob a tomb? Entered a sacred place without reading a prayer?"

"I am an explorer... I am looking for artifacts," Phillip mumbled.

"So, you might have found something. Something that belonged to an important person." They were both walking up silently for a while, thinking.

"What might it be?" asked Phillip carefully. The man smiled.

"I guess you have an idea what it might be." The smile disappeared immediately. "If I were you I would not risk staying here for another night. Nobody knows what may happen."

Phillip stopped and the man turned to him.

"I'd better go back to the camp and pack my things," he said. "Go without me!"

He waved to the tall man and rushed back as if his life depended on the time he spent on this walk. The tall man chuckled and put his hands in his pockets.

“Curses, hah.” He smiled and spat aside. “Love telling this joke every time.”

Phillip ran for his life. Literally. Grasping and stumbling, he burst into the tent he had slept in the other night and grabbed his backpack. He unzipped one of the pockets and pulled out a medallion with a half-broken ruby inside. The explorer got out of the tent and ran down the hills to the jungles. He was not scared this time. In daylight the place did not look as sinister and scary. He stopped near the shore and looked on the red-colored lake. It was still, with purple and scarlet shades and orange spots where the water was shallow.

There were no birds or any of the other creatures Phillip had seen at night. He glanced at the medallion and then threw it in the lake as far as he could. The small piece of some historic archeological find landed on the surface but sank almost immediately.

“Leave me alone, please,” Phillip whispered. He stayed on the shore for another few minutes as if waiting for the answer, but nothing happened. Relieved and relaxed, the man turned back to the camp when he heard something slapping the surface of the water. He turned back and almost cried in fear. The flamingo, the ugly, half-rotten bird he had seen the other night was holding the medallion in its bony opened beak.

The next moment it closed its muzzle and gulped, forcing the medallion inside its body. Phillip could see the shining ruby falling inside the chest of the bird, getting stuck between its ribs.

"Leave me alone!" Phillip cried. He fell backwards, his journal falling from his backpack. His last thoughts of his two girls as he scribbled on the pages.

* * *

"There's nothing more?" Annie said, with a note of loss in her voice.

I flicked through the rest of the pages- blank. "That's it. Dad's last words were to us, that he loved us, and he was sorry. That's a lot more than what most people get. C'mon," I ushered for her to get up. We couldn't waste any more time in this attic.

As I went to put the journal back in the box, I suddenly felt something heavy. It dropped to the ground with a thud before either of us could make it out. The sun light from the window shone on it, reflecting a red beam that blinded us.

The ruby was whole, broken no more, and gleamed brightly.

THE ROOM

By K.A. Dutton

It rains lightly in the courtyard of my university accommodation. I take a slow drag of my fag, trapped in a dreamland trance. Wondering if each rain drop was a soul, what life would they have. To be on top of the clouds, watching from the greatest view there is. Laying on the soft cotton, controlling the powerful winds and hearing lightning crackle beside my ears, witnessing the wave of clouds as they unleash heaven's rage.

"Can you spare a light?" A girl, plastered with two inches of makeup, pulls me back to reality.

I would usually become overly aware that it's 3 in the afternoon and I am still in my night gown, but I have this thing called not caring. My skin itches at the thought of that much makeup suffocating my skin, *you're not going anywhere girl, let it breathe.*

"Sure." I wasn't going to be that dick with a cig in my mouth and refuse to let someone use my lighter for two seconds.

As I take my final drag, I imagine the smoke circling inside me like my own personal storm cloud. It scratches the back of my throat and stains my breath. What would Ina say if she found out I spent half of my student loan on such a 'filthy' habit.

The girl smiles as she passes my lighter back to me, I give her a nod as I put my fag out and head towards Block 8 to see Jamie.

Jamie's room was only on the third floor, but I am really going to take the stairs? Nope. I would rather wait a good two minutes for the ancient elevator to take me up. I open his flat door and I'm immediately pounded with a stench only a group of four boys could make. A mix of B.O. and dirty dishes that haven't been washed since their Mums' dropped them off. One of them even just puts the dirty dish back in his cupboard. It's kind of a talent, I guess. I bet if they had the keys for the empty fifth room that they would hide dirty dishes in there too.

Jamie was waiting in bed for me. His grin was enough of a reason to look forward to the day. He wore his oversized black and red checked shirt, a black vest with some band logo and loose jeans. His skin was pale in contrast to my olive, his eyes blue compared to my brown, and his hair shone gold in the weak sunlight. But in his eyes, I was perfect, just as he was in mine.

He never minds my smokers' breath as I kiss him, a nice big exaggerated smooch that made my lips tingle. All the energy I needed for the day was suddenly in reach. That was our thing though, over-playing the PDA and making fun of the couples that do, whilst we become them. Ironic until it becomes iconic.

I slouch against him, embracing my double chin as I checked on my cats in *Neko Atsume* and he hogs the TV playing *Call of Duty*.

He glances at me during a break. Taking a few seconds just to make sure that I'm not bored or needing attention. "You okay?"

"Just perfect." I peck his cheek and ruffle his hair a little. There's no place I would rather be.

He kisses my forehead and carries on playing.

I trace my fingers lightly across his skin, stroking letters and spelling words, often consisting of 'I hope you lose' and demands like 'make me food'. His skin smells rich and warm, like dark chocolate, and I want to kiss every inch of it.

When he sleeps next to me, his eyes shut, I wonder what he dreams about. If he dreams of knights and dragons, or soldiers and war; if he thinks about warlocks and magic, or ships at sea and pirates. When he scrunches his face and burrows his eyebrows, is he fighting a monster or chasing a rabbit. Does he dream of being the lead in a world-famous band, shouting to the crowd and singing until his lungs burst or is he the drummer that no one knows the name of.

Or, like me, does he dream of the moments like these, where time pauses, and the sun has fallen, where I'm alone but graced with his presence.

And I am frozen in the reverie of love.

Outside of Jamie's window, the courtyard is nearly pitch black. Illuminated by a few outdoor lights, just bright enough for me to see the room when the curtains are left open. I reach out to find Jamie isn't in the bed with me. The bathroom light isn't on, so I know he's not in there. But he's not one to have a midnight snack run either.

The flat is unusually quiet for a home of nocturnal boys. There's a few empty food wrappers littered on the floor of the hall and two bags of rubbish that is waiting for someone to lose the short straw to drag it down to the bins. I go to text Jamie, asking where he is when I hear a faint throbbing. Or is it a thudding? No, it's more of a drumming.

The door to the 5th room is open. A small slit shows the inside of the dark room, complete darkness, as if I was staring directly into space. It casts a breeze that grazes my bare legs, sending a shiver down my spine. What on earth could Jamie be doing in there?

"Don't go in."

I spin round, trapping myself against the kitchen door, Jamie's face an inch away from mine.

"Holy crap! What are you doing?"

"I heard a noise, coming from the room. It woke me up."

"So?"

"It said my name."

"It's probably one of your flatmates."

"It was a girl," he says. His eyes are wide and alert, scared even. I have never seen him like this before.

"I've had enough of this." I'm not scared anymore. Just angry. It bubbles inside me, forcing my body to move. I slam the door shut and hear the click of the lock on the other side and the drumming stops. "There, now can we go back to bed please?"

But I hesitate. The uneasy feeling crawls underneath my skin. I tell my body to turn, to walk away, to go back to the safety of Jamie's room. But I'm frozen and my eyes can't leave the 5th room as if waiting for something to happen.

"Kristina?" Jamie whispers, he tries to pull me away. "How about we leave the flat? Let's go to the library. Let's grab our shoes and come back when we've calmed down. Yeah?"

I hear it again. The drumming. Faintly, like it's muffled.

"Do you hear that?" I say.

"Hear what?" Jamie is getting frustrated now. His hold on me starts to hurt. "Let's go, Kris."

It's getting louder. My eyes are still fixated on the door. I'm trapped in that second when a soldier sees a grenade and his mind is processing that something awful is going to happen, but his body can't respond in time, and I'm trapped, waiting for this door to open, waiting for something unholy and unnatural to explode into the claustrophobic hallway. I can feel the itchiness of my hair sticking to the sweat at the back of my neck and the tears fighting to be released as I squint harder to keep them in.

I don't want to be trapped. I don't want to wait for the inevitable.

I open the door.

I'm not sure when I decided to walk through, or when the door shut behind me. Or even when the door vanished. But it wasn't there anymore. Neither was Jamie.

I was alone in this darkness. No glimpse of light to follow, no sound other than the ringing in my ears. My shirt started to feel tight and it began to feel like I wasn't wearing anything at all. I was vulnerable. There was no taste on my tongue, just dryness. The sweat has left me too, and my heart is pumping at a steady rate. I'm having a panic attack in my mind without the physical responses.

"Jamie!" I call out. I must find him.

We always talked about these situations. What we would do if the zombie apocalypse happened, if aliens attacked, if demons were after us. We laughed when we planned them. I don't think we're laughing anymore. It would be nicer if I knew what the *fuck* was happening though.

"JAMIE!" I scream. I'm running. Running into nothing, running to nowhere. But I must do something.

Suddenly, my body is catapulted into the air, I land on what feels like concrete. Something runs down my face as I try to sit up. Still no light, so I'm guessing it's blood. Hopefully nothing too serious. *Like hell* was I going to die in this place from a fall, that would be pathetic.

But what did I trip over? It feels heavy.

"Kristina?" It chokes. "Oh god, Kristina."

I feel for his shirt, it's soaking. "Jamie?" I cry. I know it's him, I know it's his voice, I know it's his shirt, but I don't want it to be him. If this is blood that he's drenched in, there's too much for anyone to lose. "What happened?"

His breaths are haggard and shallow, but he responds. "I don't know- I think I've been here for days. Someone- something, keeps attacking me. Jesus Christ, Kris, I can't see a thing. I-"

"-Shh, it's fine. Everything is fine. I'm going to get us out of here, okay?" I know it's getting harder for him to breathe, and it's hurting him to talk. But if he's been here days, how long have I been in here? Days as well? No, he sounds too certain of the time. But if I only just arrived, then who was the Jamie I left behind the door?

I can't think about that now.

I need a plan.

Jamie said there's something that comes out of the darkness and attacks him. So, I wait. It's the best choice, as I can't leave Jamie behind. The exit, if there even is one, may be far. I can't carry Jamie for longer than two minutes and I can't leave him behind to die. We're going to ride or die together, that's the rule.

I'm knelt beside Jamie, the blood slowly sticking to my feet. Grim.

"Can you spare a light?" A voice echoes, it's familiar. "Do you remember me?"

And then there is light. From my own lighter, in the hands of someone I saw for a minute in the courtyard.

She isn't wearing makeup anymore, or anything for that matter. She is stark naked, but her body isn't completely human, she is paper white and smooth with the figure of a woman but drags along something that looks big. Wings. Featherless, like a bat. I look to her eyes, pupils took up all the space, but I knew they were staring into mine. She grins, her mouth slowly spreading further and further until it takes up half her face, displaying a hundred sharp, bloody, teeth.

I can't feel anything. I can't feel temperature, I can't smell anything, I can't taste anything. I can't move. My breath releases a frozen cloud making the fire from my lighter flicker.

"Let's make a deal, shall we?" She jumps up effortlessly, and lands silently, as if her feet aren't even touching the ground. The lighter is still in her hand, but it starts to get brighter.

"What kind of deal?" I say.

"Him," she points. "I want him. I keep him. I let you leave."

I turn to Jamie, truly seeing how bad of a condition he is in now there was light. His shirt is torn to show the bite marks in his chest leaking blood. I stroke his soft face, a face that I have kissed a million times over. He scrunches it in pain. "No," I whisper.

"No?" She kneels on the other side of Jamie and runs her long nails across his torso. "I won't kill him."

My eyes left Jamie to meet hers. "No." I say firmly. "You can fuck right off and get your own man."

She guffaws, clutching her stomach and pretending to fall to the ground. "Oh, honey. You'll give him up, they all do."

"How about we play a game instead?"

"No thanks," I say. Games with demons never end well.

She sobs, "Pretty please?" Switching back to her grinning face in a split second. "If you win, you both get to leave, and he will be magically healed like this never even happened."

"If I lose?"

"I'll be nice. I'll let you leave. But I get to keep him," she purrs. "It's an easy game. Just guess what kind of demon I am."

"What kind of demon you are?"

"You'll know it. I'm quite famous in your world. You have one guess."

When did I agree to this? How did we even get into this mess? Why us?

Jamie is unresponsive, not even aware about the plans of this demon.

He won't even know that you gave him up.

But I'll know. I wouldn't be able to live with myself. I must win this game. She could be a vampire. But why the fascination with only Jamie? Why am I not bleeding out on the floor right now too?

Because you're a girl!

And what demons seek out men?

I lean over and kiss Jamie's frozen lips, taking a second to memorize the lines in his face. "I love you," I whisper in his ear. "I love you so bloody much."

I stand tall, brushing the hair from my face, and face her. "You're a Succubus." I say.

Her face sinks, she loses her grin, and releases a shriek. I'm thrown back, the air hitting me like a truck.

The last thing I see is the girl turning towards a silhouette. "Your turn." She grins.

Suddenly, the array of light and colours smacks me. I'm in a room. I'm back in Jamie's room. It takes a moment for my eyes to adjust.

The clock on the wall reads 3:34pm and sunlight pours through the open window. I must have been right but there was something nagging at me.

Jamie is on the bed, reading a comic book. He isn't bleeding anymore, not even a drop on him. He's okay. "You're back! What took you so long?" He grins, his gorgeous grin that usually opens a thousand fireflies loose inside me.

But it doesn't. Why don't I feel the fireflies?

This isn't Jamie.

THE ASYLUM

By Shannan Mitchener

INTERVIEW ROOM 4

"Hello, my name's Luke Shelley and my friends were murdered last night at Redcrest Asylum."

I'd barely taken a sip of coffee and sat down at my desk when he burst in; drenched in blood that dripped steadily on the cream tile between the front door of the station and the reception desk. His eyes were wild, his hair stuck up at every angle, his mouth pressed into a hard line, and his fists had slammed onto the desk with grim finality.

"Can you spell that for me?" Detective Poe asks.

He fidgets uncomfortably in the metal chair, pulling dead skin from his blood-stained fingernails. It's heavily oxidised, leaving it a stale burgundy colour. He looks up at Detective Poe and I can see the fear in his young eyes.

"Yeah, it's Luke Shelley, S-H-E-L-L-E-Y."

His quiet voice echoes around the basic room. A metal table, four plastic chairs, pale yellow walls. One window. High up. Too small for a person, barely large enough to let the rising sun shine through. It's difficult not to feel claustrophobic in here - even for me.

Poe presses 'record' on the tape recorder lying ominously between them. "This is Officer Campbell, Officer Hill, and Detective Poe interviewing Luke Shelley in interview room 4 on the 26th of June, 2011. The time is 5:47AM. Luke, tell us what happened."

Luke nods, biting at his lower lip furiously as he stares at his warped reflection in the smudged metal of the table.

REDCREST ASYLUM

The asylum looked ominous under the moon. Short and derelict, there were about five stout buildings spread in a semi-circle straight ahead of us. I felt like someone was watching us, but maybe that was just the way the windows seemed to glare with their glass eyelashes and empty irises.

The barricaded door read 'ABANDON ALL HOPE YE WHO ENTER HERE'. We nervously laughed it off and broke through, we become engulfed in a cloud of dust. Rust burned my nose each time I inhaled. Graffiti and rubbish littered the peeling walls and dirty floors, so derelict they looked more like ash than concrete.

We climbed the stairs slowly, listening to every creak underneath our uneasy feet. Ollie coughed, and then laughed when we jumped.

You think you know what darkness is when you shut off the light in your bedroom at night, but this was something else. This was heavy darkness, bursting with things hiding in the shadows. I was glad to turn the lantern in when we'd sat down in the room at the end of the corridor.

"So what now?" Ollie asked.

"Asylum selfie?" I suggested.

We all sat, cross legged, in the middle of the room, as I angled the camera to take a picture. We all snorted with laughter as we twisted our faces to look at scared as possible, and the sound bounced off of the walls of the dingy cell. The flash made my heart race – I always worry I'll get a glimpse of something that shouldn't be there.

As Ollie and Rory began to unfurl the sleeping bags, I uploaded the photo to Facebook, and only seconds later someone commented.

That guy in the corner is soooo creepy! Who is that? Thought it was just you three going out tonight?

“Hey, Rory, your sister thinks she’s funny,” I snickered, tossing him the phone. His face glowed warmly from the screen, a smile spreading across his face. He rolled his eyes at me.

“So scary,” he laughed, wiggling his fingers sarcastically.

Ollie set his phone up so we could watch Netflix, and suddenly it didn’t seem so scary anymore with the sound of a studio audience roaring with laughter.

My phone kept buzzing with comments on the photo, all of them pretty much the same – everyone asking about the ‘person’ in the corner. I tap out an angry reply:

I can’t see anyone there. Good one guys, you’re so funny.

A few minutes later someone had commented with a copy of the photo, a red circle drawn around the top left.

Then who’s that?

I squinted, but I still couldn’t see anything.

I woke up in the night, and after a moment of panicked fumbling I found the lantern and switched it back on, only to find that the room was empty.

“Hello?” I called into the desolate corridor. I took measured steps, each one echoing off of the decaying walls. The windows were cracked and even smashed in some places, revealing only the moon and a black sea of grass.

On the last step down the stairs, my foot found something soft, and the light revealed a hat. Rory's hat. I felt sick. And then more so when I saw something dark on my fingers. There was thick scarlet blood coating the hat, coating my hands and making everything sticky and warm. I retched violently, throwing the hat far away in horror.

My breaths were loud and fast as I walked, fast paced but controlled, out of the door and into the field. I hurried in that way you might hurry back to your bedroom in the dark. You know if you run or look behind you then you're admitting that there could be something chasing you.

"Hello?!" I shouted, looking around desperately. And suddenly from behind me, I became very aware of the sound of running. I whipped around just in time for Ollie to tackle me to the ground.

"Luke!" He cried.

"What's- where's Rory? What's wrong?"

"We came outside for a piss and, and this guy at the bottom of the stairs... we thought he was a guard or something, but he... he stabbed Rory, man, he stabbed Rory." Ollie was openly crying, but when I offered a hand in comfort he pushed me away and stood up. "We ran outside, I'm sorry man, but Rory was hurt and we needed to get out of there, I'm so sorry for leaving you..."

I would have done the same thing.

"But he caught us. He grabbed Rory and I just... I didn't know what to do. I'm such a fucking pussy, I just left him." Ollie turned away from me and paces five steps away, then back.

"We need to call the police," I told him, my voice strangled. My phone was on the grass, and, of course, smashed. "Give me your phone."

Ollie laughed, too loudly. "I don't have it on me," he said, his voice getting higher. "We used Rory's for the light, I left mine in my sleeping bag."

"I'll go get it," I said, regretting the words instantly.

"No, Luke. We go in together."

I didn't argue.

Ollie grabbed my hand as we stepped inside. I didn't say anything, just squeezed it as we walked into the pitch black building together. I climbed the stairs first, feeling my way by lightly tracing my fingers against the rough walls. Ollie's hand was still clenched in my sweaty fist, and the grip got tighter and tighter as we continued down the corridor. The light from the lantern glowed softly through the door.

We weren't alone.

Someone was stood in the far left corner. I didn't miss the glint of a knife in his hand, and from the way Ollie's breath hitched, neither did he.

I couldn't tell you what he looked like. I couldn't tell you what he was wearing. But I can tell you what sound Ollie made when the knife plunged into him. I could describe the way Ollie looked at me as the man pulled it out. I could show you exactly how Ollie folded, crumpled into my arms like a puppet with cut strings.

I'm ashamed to tell you that I dropped him. I'm not proud that I ran, faster than I've ever done in my life. I ran until I hit lit streets and the rising sun, until Redcrest Asylum was far behind me.

THE PHOTO

"That is not you!" Poe doesn't shout. Doesn't need to. I avoid looking at anyone as they argue about the photo Poe has just found.

Instead I focus on the paint flakes on the far wall. *What a stupid decision*, I think, *to paint a room such as an interrogation room in a police station white.* White, which shows all evidence of blood, sick, and piss. White which decays so quickly, which discolours in sun exposure, which exhibits water damage from the surrounding leaky copper pipes.

"Yes it is! What do you mean, 'that's not me'?!" Luke argues, his voice louder but weaker.

"Mr Shelley, that looks nothing like you. I don't understand how-"

"That is me! Who else would it be?!" Luke's forefinger points accusingly at the photo, at the third person in the picture with Ollie and Rory.

The photo looks exactly how I pictured it, except of course that Luke is not there. There is another man in his place. If anyone in this room were to pretend to be this boy, I would have the best chance. We share the thick blonde hair, blue eyes, white skin. Luke is black, and even if that weren't enough evidence, he has a thick scar on his cheek, which the boy in the photo is quite clearly missing.

"Jamie Hitchcock, actually. Mr Shelley. Someone the parents of Rory and Ollie identified as one of their friends. Oddly enough, they had no idea who you were." He pauses, jerks his head at me so I can see the screen, see the part of the photo he is pointing to. "That, however, is you."

There is a blurry shape in the top left corner of the photo. The detective deftly switches to another window to show us that corner magnified, lightened, sharpened, and we can all very plainly see Luke's face, staring at the boys.

"Are you joking?!" Luke asks, a humourless laugh escaping his lips. He leans back in his chair, runs a hand through his hair. The blood on his shirt is more prominent than ever, and we do not miss it. "That's not me, I look nothing like that. That's insane."

"Yes," Poe says pointedly. "Insane."

THE DISAPPEARANCE

Campbell went to the asylum, leaving me behind to do paperwork. I would be lying if I said I wasn't relieved. He returns in a foul mood, marches to the cells with me scurrying behind him.

"WHERE IS HE?"

He throws open the door to the cell Luke had been placed in for holding, but by the look on his face, there is no-one in there. He leans back against the cold brick wall and sighs, runs a hand through his sparse hair.

"What did you find at the asylum?" I ask, a low murmur.

"We found the boys. Dead, unfortunately."

The grey linoleum beneath my feet distorts violently as my stomach backflips. "Dead?"

"Stabbed, just like Shelley said. We found the body of Jamie, too. The boy Luke claimed to be." His voice oozes sarcasm. "He was in the cell, still in his sleeping bag. But we found something very... unsettling."

I am holding my breath.

"We looked at the pictures we took before leaving, Campbell, I swear we did. The photo we took of that cell where they'd stayed, there was nothing there that shouldn't have been. I checked the photo myself, and again in the car on our way back." Poe stares at me with such intensity I am tempted to look away. "The kid, Luke. I don't know how, but he was there. Standing in that cell. Top left corner, just like he was in the other picture."

"He was there?" My voice is barely a whisper.

"Yep. So we raced back of course, sirens going, we sprint across that damned field and get up those stairs as fast as we can, and he's gone." Poe's face looks tired, pale. "And he's not here. I want every single officer and station in this area given a photo of Shelley and a briefing. We now need him questioned in relation to the murders of Oliver Straub, Rory King, and James Hitchcock."

RESEARCH

Detective Poe is at his desk. He's currently on the phone to Rory's mother, having just finished talking to Ollie's. He's told them the news, and I swear I could hear their grief from here. Poe sighs after hanging up and rubs his nose, then catches me watching and shoots me a sad smile. "Never gets easier, kid." He picks up the phone again, begins calling Jamie's parents, ready to start all over again.

I turn away, unwilling to watch him go through it again.

Luke Shelley's patient file stares at me from the computer monitor. The photo once again looks nothing like him aside from the matching scar down his cheek.

He was admitted in 1935 at the age of nineteen. His father abused him and took photographs of it. Some of these photos are attached to the file. Even in black and white they are gruesome. Not quite as gruesome, though, as the picture of Luke's father.

David Shelley was beaten to death with his camera by his son while he slept. When questioned, Luke had no memory of the incident, and no memory of himself. '*Extensive memory loss as a result of deep emotional and physical abuse/trauma*'.

I look further, and eventually come to a heading called *Therapy*.

Doctor Burke, head of Psychological Trauma ward, recommends therapies that may trigger the patient's memory.

Doctor Peters and Doctor Samson begin therapy on the 10th of May 1935, two weeks after admission. Photos are taken of the patient. He gets upset, though when asked why, he responds that he does not know. He is confused, and more photos distress him further.

21/5/1935. Sixth treatment. Patient requests we take no photos. We take more this time. He seems agitated.

23/5/1935. Seventh treatment. Doctor Peters stimulates Shelley with a cane to the back while Doctor Samson takes pictures. Patient is very vocal and responds negatively to the therapy. Afterwards when asked how he felt, he is upset and tearful. We ask if he remembers anything before the institute, and he says no.

The 'therapies' get more and more violent. Eventually the doctors are beating Luke openly with their fists, pulling his hair, even at one point breaking his fingers.

26th of June 1935. Thirteenth treatment. Usual routine is executed, this time with a metal pipe. Unfortunately, as Doctor Peters attempted to hit patient with object, patient fell to his knees and was hit on the rear of the skull. Patient pronounced dead, incident ruled an accident.

I don't want to believe it, although I think I already do. This is the same Luke Shelley. But I know I have to do my own research, find out more about this. There's no way he escaped holding without the notice of an entire police station or entered and then left a crime scene undetected. Not if he's human.

No-one notices as I grab my coat and leave.

FIELD WORK

The asylum itself is terrifying, but the windows frighten me more than anything. They reveal nothing except a thick void; so black and deep that I am unsure if I will even find anything inside. I go in anyway.

It is still light outside, barely, but it is black like night in the concrete rooms. I feel like at any moment I might be swallowed whole, never to be seen again. I don't miss the unmistakable stench of blood in the air.

"Luke?" I call out. "Luke? It's Officer Hill. Are you okay? Do you need help?"

My voice echoes off of the black walls and bounces back to me with no response, but I notice a sign above me which has been wiped clear of the dust. *Psychological Trauma Ward*. I swallow, and suddenly am sure of everything – this is where Luke died. This is where I will find him.

When I reach the top of the stairs I am alarmed to see that the sun is gone. I'd been outside minutes ago and the sun was warm on my back. Now my bone-white knuckles tremble as I slowly head towards the last room in the corridor.

There is blood on the floor, and my stomach drops a few feet at the sight of it. It all seems far too real now, and I long to turn back. But I can't.

"Luke?" I ask, my voice breaking. I shine the light through in the room and am almost unsurprised when I see him in the corner. His back is to me. "Luke."

In a moment that seems to go by in slow-motion, he turns around. He doesn't look at me, is instead staring at the ground, but his palms face outwards and they are covered in blood. I swallow. He lifts his hands, stares blankly as he turns them this way and that. Then he says something.

"What?" I say softly.

"Whose blood is this?" He asks me. He finally looks at me, and his face is so pained I falter, lower the torch ever so slightly.

"I don't know," I whisper. "Come on, come with me," I tell him, gesturing to him. "We'll fix this, we'll-"

"Yes," he says with such finality I am taken aback. His face is blank, his jaw set, his mouth a hard line. Then it breaks into a grim smile. "We can."

Then he breaks into a sprint towards me.

19 YEARS LATER

Officer Stoker had barely taken a sip of coffee and sat down at his desk when the man burst in; his police uniform drenched in blood that dripped steadily on the cream tile. His blue eyes were wild, his blonde hair pointed at odd angles, his mouth pressed into a hard line that distorted the scar on his cheek. His fists slammed onto the desk between them with grim finality.

"Hello, my name's Luke Shelley and my friends were murdered last night at Redcrest Asylum."

THE BASEMENT

By K.A. Dutton

[*Ryan Lamport sits alone in a darkroom built in the basement of his Mother's home in Manchester. It's 1:26am as he marvels over his photography. The photographs feature a woman in various settings.*]

I don't sleep much these days. Too much to do, too much see. My life is hectic at the moment. Just one big mess. I have my Mum nagging me. *When are you going to get a job? When will you be more grown up? When will you move out? I'm worried about you.* She always ends it on that sentence. *I'm worried about you.* There's nothing to worry about. I do have a job- I'm a photographer. Do I make money? Not yet. She just doesn't understand. Photography is an art, it's intimate. I can't sell what I have anyway, it's a piece of me, *she's* a piece of me.

Natalie Erikson.

Mum is still persistent though. I swear, she doesn't even listen to me. Now and again she makes me go for interviews. I have one later today. Maybe I should get some sleep... Nah. There's too much on my mind. I wish for many things at the minute, but I do wish my Mum would just leave me be. I'll move out eventually. I'm just working things out with Natalie. I mean, we'll get a house or apartment together eventually. I hope. I don't know. But I do wish for it too. I love Natalie, and I want to have a life with her. I'm not sure if she wants the same though. Mum is always telling me: *bring that Natalie girl over. Let her meet the family. We haven't even seen her once. Is she nice to you? Is she pretty? Does she have a job? Why don't you have a job?* Again, usually ending with that question. She annoys me so much. Treating me like I'm not an adult. When I turn away, I feel like she's judging me. Thinking Natalie isn't real, just because I have never brought her home.

I'm so frustrated that I have another interview. They never like me. What's the point in wasting time with all that when I could be doing something worthwhile? Like taking photos, getting out in the world, spending precious time with Natalie. The last interview was to work at Tesco. How degrading. I have a *career*. I have skills. I can't waste those skills working on the tills like some teenager saving up for a car or university. I don't want to be stuck in a dead-end job, what would Natalie think? She wouldn't want to marry someone who works at such a low-grade job. She deserves better. I deserve better. I need to make enough money to make her happy. To treat her the way she needs to be treated. Like the good boyfriend, I'll be.

I hope you can see my point, I apologise for babbling on. I've just been so angry lately. Natalie and I aren't talking as much. She's busy. She's busy a lot these days. I would appreciate it if she made some time for me, like I would do for her. Like what I am doing for her. But I can't stay angry. I love her. I have loved her since secondary school. She's the love of my life. Oh, I just must tell you the story.

We were in Maths together, Year 10. I was at a big school, and I don't think I ever had a class with her before that. Naturally, I saw her a few times around the school, but I never *noticed* her. So yes, we were in Maths. Luckily, I was placed on the table behind hers. I still remember it vividly. The smell of her hair. It was long back then. Nearly meeting her waist. Straight, and a lighter brown. These days she has it curled, with a few highlights, and just above her shoulders. She suited both styles in my opinion. Mr Michaels was in his early 60's and had perfected the monotone voice. Even when he shouted for the class to calm down we couldn't take it seriously. It could drive anyone to sleep. I'm sure you had a teacher like that at your school too. Anyway. Natalie's pen rolled off her desk and onto the carpet. It was close to me, so I reached down to get it and caught her gaze. She looked at me, in the eyes, and smiled. That was the moment. All I could think was, *she's so beautiful. She smiled at me. She looked at me!* And the touch of her hands. The touch. So warm and delicate. I was in awe.

Oh, Natalie.

You can guess what I spent the rest of secondary school doing. The years before we finished, I was fated to be in half of her classes. I was obsessed with her. With trying to talk to her, catching her attention, getting her to like me. She was my life. I got into photography though in College. She had gone to the one cross town sadly. I was tempted to transfer but they didn't do my course. We never confirmed it, but I feel like our relationship started for real after college. She had just got her job at Costa, she still works there now. We hung out more, spent our days together, did everything really. She was the girl I could take home to the Mother you know? *Could* being the key word if my Mum wasn't so nosey.

It was our first date. Our first real date, to me anyway. We went to the cinema to watch *The Roommate.* I had no clue what it was about. I mean, Natalie picked it so I just went with what she wanted to watch. I wasn't one to argue and risk ruining the first date. I didn't really understand the movie. I'm not into thrillers or horrors or whatever it was meant to be. I think Natalie enjoyed it, but she did check her phone a lot, which was a little rude. After the movie, we took the long walk home. It was such a calm night. You could really see the stars.

I'm glad I'm talking about it. You always feel better when you reflect on things. We're going through some hiccups at the moment. It's been rough, I'm not going to lie. She's just been so so so busy, so we don't have time to see each other as often as we used to. Sometimes, I don't even know where she is. I was at our usual restaurant the other week. I needed to get out of the house and couldn't stand another night with Mum.

Natalie was there.

With another guy.

I couldn't believe it. I was shocked. Hurt. Devastated, even. I thought we told each other everything and we were open with each other. But I've never seen this guy before. Where did he come from? How long have they been talking? Was she cheating on me? They were laughing, and enjoying their food. I didn't know what to do. I grabbed a table close to them, but far enough. Catching bits of conversation. I couldn't process it though. My heart was going crazy in my chest. I was sweating. I ordered some food but couldn't eat it. I loved Natalie. I thought she loved me.

We were going to move in together, have a house, have children. Everything. I didn't order dessert.

What would you do in that situation? I went through all the possibilities. Maybe it's a cousin, her work friend, or he's just pestering her. Natalie couldn't betray me. Reminding myself of that calmed me down. I followed them home, they were walking back to hers. Natalie has such a big house. Big open garden. I knew then that I didn't have anything to worry about. They both entered the house. I mean, Natalie has never taken me to meet her parents. So, if she was cheating on me, it would be crazy to introduce the cheater to her parents. I mean, c'mon. I knew I could trust her. It had to be a family member. Who else could it be?

When I went home that night, Mum told me about the interview I have later. She was so proud of herself. Saying things like *this is a good chance for you Ryan. Be more like your brother. Look how happy he is.* I couldn't catch a break. I was tempted to just not go to the interview. What's the point? Things are already bad with Natalie, I would blame myself if I had a full-time job that took away more time for us. Mum always has to bring up Ben. Always comparing us. *He moved out when he was only 20* she would say. *He is successful, married, and has a respectable job. You could have that too if you stop obsessed over your photography and that girl.*

She just can't accept the differences between us. Have you ever felt like you were in the shadow of someone you know? I've always been that shadow. The shadow of my brother. He would tease me about Natalie. *When are you guys going to sleep together? Have you even kissed yet? Is she even real?*

So, what if we've not done those things yet. Natalie and I are taking it slow. I know she's shy. She's quiet. She doesn't want to rush into anything. Everyone at school was obsessed with it. Having sex. All losing it early. Bet most of them regret it now. Natalie and I are going to have a special first time. It'll be magical. And something we can remember, and know we waited for it. It won't be a spur of the moment thing. Anyway, Ben isn't as perfect as Mum thinks. I know for a *fact* he's been cheating on his wife. He even brags about it. Making fun of all the times he's done it more than me. Teasing that I'm a virgin. I can't wait for it to come out. I've been tempted on more than one occasion to tell everyone. I mentioned it to Mum once, she didn't believe me and told me to stop talking about it. I wonder if she already knows. The oh-so-perfect son, not very perfect now, is he? At least I have a career I enjoy. I would hate to be stuck behind a desk and call that being successful. Rotting in a chair, blinding myself behind a computer screen for 9 hours a day.

Natalie is the only thing good in my life. She keeps me going. Thinking of her, makes me invincible. I can put up with my Mum and Ben, knowing Natalie is in my life. Whispering in my limited dreams the life we'll have together. Leaving everyone else behind. That'll show them. When I'm old and Ben is divorced, probably on to a second or third wife. I'll be the one with the better life. A successful life with the woman I truly love. I don't know what I would do without her. It makes me cry sometimes. If Natalie wasn't in my life. If she didn't love me. What kind of life would I have?

The other day we were walking in the park. I hadn't seen her in so long. I couldn't get too close though because her dog didn't like me. He was a yapper. I didn't want to startle Natalie. Kids were playing on the swings, and the slides, making a right ruckus. I couldn't help imagining what our kids would be like. I would ideally like two, a girl and a boy. Everyone wants one of each right? I would name them Jake and Alice, if I had a choice. Natalie would probably suggest better ones. She's so smart and how could I argue with the mother of my children? Anyway, we were at the park. Reaching the lake where we would go as teenagers to feed the ducks. When out of nowhere this guy comes up and kisses Natalie! The nerve. I wanted to protect her, to run to her, to fight this stranger but

I couldn't get close because of her dog. I couldn't see who the guy was but he didn't stay for long. First the guy at the restaurant, now the horny stranger in the park? I need to be more protective over Natalie, I'm so worried about her. She won't tell me how she's feeling but I can't help but imagine. I wish I could be with her all the time. I wish we had time for each other. I wish her dog liked me so I could have gone up to her and given her a shoulder to cry on. She's been going through a tough time and I'm just sitting here complaining about my life instead. I have been so selfish.

Yesterday, I went to visit her at work. Costa was as busy as always. Natalie was hard at work behind the till. She was so quick. I can't believe she's been working there as long as she has. She deserves better. I've captured some amazing shots of her in the café though. It's like magic when she's so focused. She's never even noticed the camera before. I think she's embarrassed when I take photos. And seeing me visit her at work. She never serves me. It's always some other woman that will never be as beautiful as Natalie. She asked what I'll be having. Then it came to me that I was completely zoned out. I didn't even look at the menu. I stuttered and froze. How embarrassing. I asked for a Cinnamon Latte, and they said they would bring it over.

I got a seat by the window. Still in sight of Natalie. Her hair was up in a bun, barely any makeup. That's another thing I love about her. Natural beauty. Not fussed with the makeup generation of women today. Plastering themselves with layers of foundation. Gross. I could tell when Natalie was making my order. My heart skipped a beat as she walked over to me. Placing it in front of me. She didn't meet my eyes though. I asked her how she was doing. She joked and asked what my name was. I guess we've been so busy, we're like strangers now. She didn't stay for long though, back to work! The Latte was nice. But how could it not be when Natalie made it? I said thank you when I left, but she didn't even look up. She whispered something to the girl that served me on the till, who did look at me weirdly. Maybe she's jealous.

It's almost 3am. Maybe I should try and sleep. I wonder when I'll see Natalie again. I can't stand it. She'll be fast asleep right now. I wonder if she's dreaming of me. I hope she is. Even though we don't see each other often enough. At least I have enough photos of her to remind me. I'm so proud of all my photography of her. She's such a good model. So natural. That's the thing about photography. The best subjects are ones that don't even realise they are on camera.

THE ROAD

By K.A. Dutton

In every town there is a road that is famous for its record of accidents. The accidents in question, are usually the result of bad designing, road neglect, or generally due to assholes who think they are above the law. The only 'solutions' that would be put in place would be new signs for slower speeds, hedges being trimmed, and installation of street lights that should have been planted there years before. Or, the road would be eradicated entirely to make room for something new. It eventually gets forgotten and left behind. Not even a story worthy of the history books.

My forgotten road had a rich history of fatal accidents. Even long before I came into existence. The first one I remember, happened when I was 5.

We were on our way home; our house was just around the corner. I could see the lights of the ambulance pouring through the window that I couldn't reach yet. There was a lot of noise and it made my brother very excited.

"Do you think anyone has died?" He asked. Mum was driving at the time, but her eyes were darting around for any details she could spill in the morning when she meets the girls for breakfast.

"Hopefully not, dear."

But of course, hardly anyone escaped from the clutches of death on this road. It was as if the road was built above Satan's office.

The car had completely lost control, crashing into the brick wall and toppling over. It crushed the driver and the passenger inside. A Grandfather, and his grandson that I quickly found out was a boy in my year at school. I can't remember him very well, he was in the other class, but I still feel this twinge of impending mortality when I think of him. Not even a face to put the imaginary picture to, just a faceless figure in school uniform.

There were many more to come in the years after. You just, stop taking notice. I feel bad about it but it just happened so often that most of us stopped peering through the police tape to check. We stopped fixing the dents in the wall, we stopped planting the flowers in the small section of field around it and we stopped making it the front page of our newspaper. It was barely worth a paragraph on the 5th page.

It wasn't until I was 15 that I started to pay attention again.

I have always been a firm believer in ghosts. Maybe it was because I wanted to believe in something, I'll settle for that. I had hoped that the first ghost I would see was my Dad's. Sometimes I wished it, those sometimes were every birthday after. If you have ever lost someone you know that the pain is always there. There was a moment where I realised that I had forgotten his voice. The way he carried himself. Did he kiss me goodnight? Or was that just a dream I made up for something to cling onto? I couldn't even recall my last memory of him. When I think of him as being 'passed on', there's hatred that bubbles up to the surface. How could he leave us? Wouldn't he want to stay and make sure we're okay before going to heaven? And then I would hate myself for wishing that. Death is always harder on the living.

I had just finished a long day at school. Staying behind to carry on with my GCSE art project for my coursework. It was late, dark, and the killer road was not one I would choose to walk through on a foggy night. My glasses kept steaming up as I hurried to get home, my bag was heavy as if I was pulling an anchor along the pavement. I barely made him out, and he genuinely looked like a drunk man. Not uncommon. Nothing massive to worry about.

He was hunched over but facing one of the houses leading to my street. His clothes were rugged, with a bent hat sat tall on his head, and he couldn't quite stand still. The closer I got to him, the harder it got to look at him. It was as if I was staring into white noise on a TV. He was black and white, which I thought was because he was wearing a tuxedo, but he became transparent. I caught my breath, and everything went still. *He's going to turn around and chase me. He's going to bloody kill me. I'm going to die on the road of death, and it won't even be a damn car accident.* But after a few minutes of paralyzed panicking, I crossed the street and went around him, and he didn't even twitch in the sound of my presence.

Willow, our golden angel, greeted me as soon as she heard the key turning in the door. Tail wagging like she was going to take off at any moment. She demands a solid five minutes of attention before letting you even leave the hallway. A calming cloud of comfort that made everything okay again. They say that animals are hyper sensitive to the supernatural, so if Willow was acting unusual, I think that would be the time for worrying.

"C'mon Willow." I said. It was time for dinner, and my brother was not one to rely on to feed her.

I couldn't stop staring at the road as I passed it. Many explanations racing in my head to make sense of yesterday's experience. It was probably a drunk man, and it was foggy. I already have awful sight too, that makes me an unreliable witness. But I can't stop hoping for more, even though the thought terrified me.

I planted myself on the library computer during lunch. It was fairly empty, mainly a spot for the quiet ones. The ones that needed to study for exams used the other library that was reserved for the 6th formers doing their A-levels, but they were nice to let final year GCSE students join them. This library was tiny in comparison. The lights were blindingly bright, kind of like the lights they use in hospitals and dentists. The wallpaper was tearing in the corners and featured a pale zig-zag design that hadn't been updated in decades. The computers were still using Windows 7.

The librarian had a pack of onion ring crisps beside her keyboard whilst chewing an over-stuffed sandwich, pieces of lettuce fell with each bite. On her desk were two signs, one of 'NO SHOUTING' and 'NO FOOD ALLOWED'. She whipped out a bottle of coke from her desk drawer.

It was a small enough space that the putrid smell from the sandwich made me gag. I do not like meat, meat does not like me (when it's dead, anyway). The sight and smell are vile. Give me a cheese and tomato sandwich any day.

Focus.

I logged in and immediately searched for all the accidents that took place on the road. The list that came up named enough bodies to keep our small-village graveyard relevant. It was horrific. I knew it was bad, but not *this* bad. Most died, few injured, few even left with life-changing injuries. From the list, only 5 people in the history of this road's birth, have walked away without a scratch.

I'm not sure what I was hoping to achieve from this. I think I've watched too much *Ghost Whisperer.* Waiting for something interesting, something that doesn't sound right, to happen. I could face the ghost I saw and help him move on and be spiritually changed forever. I was just hoping for something exciting to happen.

Then the bell rang, and I headed to my next class.

Thankfully it wasn't foggy on the walk home this time. But heaven's gates were open, and the rain had no mercy. I had forgotten my umbrella- again.

My uniform was quickly soaked, five minutes in my 20-minute walk, and I grimaced with each step I took in soggy socks. I accepted that I was once again, blind due to the weather because they haven't invented waterproof glasses yet. Note to self- it might be time to invest in contacts.

Do you ever find yourself so lost in thought that you don't even notice the journey? Muscle memory guides you down your usual route and my mind brings me back when I meet *the* road. Kind of like in games when they automatically save before a boss battle, I'm overly cautious as to why my mind couldn't ignore this part of my journey as it did the rest.

A few cars pass by, people finishing work, kids going home from school. But I look through the rain drops on my glasses, faintly making out a man. *Nothing to worry about Ellie, just a pedestrian.* Except he's standing still with his back facing you. I squint as hard as possible and pause for a second to clean my glasses.

I hear it before I see it, but I look up in time to see the guy in the road, a car skidding as it tries to break until it just goes right through him and crashes into the wall.

My cold fingers fumble to my pocket and I immediately call 999.

The car bonnet was like a crumpled piece of paper, and the air bags made it hard for me to see through the windows. No one was moving. There was only the driver, thankfully. I don't know if I could handle a crash with child victims.

The door opened with a hard pull, glass crunching beneath my shoes, and I climb in. A shard pierces my hand, but I ignore it.

"Sir, are you okay? Can you hear me?" I couldn't make him out very well but there were blurs of red with no response. I want to throw my glasses for being so useless. How am I supposed to help him? Are you supposed to get them out of the car or leave them where they are so you don't injury them further? I couldn't remember.

"Sir, can you hear me?" I repeat. This time reaching over to him and putting two of my fingers against his neck. "Sir?"

No pulse.

"Oh my god," I choke. Tears start to stream from my eyes and it gets harder to breath. *He's dead.* I back out of the car and fall over onto the pavement, my hands covering my mouth. *He's dead. He's dead. He's dead.*

Then I see blurs of blue and red. I looked out to see if I could see the man that caused this. The ghost. Just something to scream at. But there was no one there.

Willow wakes me by jumping onto my bed and nudging my face with her wet nose. Sunlight pours through my bedroom window, I can feel the heat radiating from it. I sit up, with hesitation, as the events of yesterday evening process.

"Oh, Willow..." I run my fingers through her fur. She looks at me with her happy eyes and wags her tail. I don't even notice that I'm missing school. I should be in my second lesson of the day by now.

My glasses were dry thankfully, giving me the gift of sight.

"Ellie!" Mum calls.

I sigh, "Let's go, Willow."

Mum has made a whole fry up of vegetarian sausages, hash browns, baked beans, fried bread, scrambled eggs, the whole works. The kitchen stinks of oil.

"Honey..." Mum pulls me towards her, holding me. "I know it's hard witnessing a crash, but you'll be okay. I called the school, so just relax and eat something, okay?" She brushes my hair behind my ears and looks at me with sad eyes.

"Okay," I reply.

I was pecking at a bit of scrambled egg when the doorbell rang. Willow jumped up, alert, ready to greet whoever it could be.

Mum was in the back, so I got up to answer it.

I was faced with a stranger, one that looked oddly inhuman. As if he was photoshopped for a magazine. His skin glowed, his hair was smooth without a stray in sight, and his teeth were like pearls when he smiled.

"Hi, are you Ellie?" He asked, his voice raised Goosebumps all over my body. Who was this guy?

"Yes, I am."

"I heard you were the one that saved me. From the crash."

I lost my breath, "But I didn't save anyone. The driver died."

The man's expression changed, for a split second, I saw the ghost in his eyes. "You must have been in shock. I'm perfectly fine, not even a scratch on me."

CHRISTMAS DINNER

By Antonio Ferrara

The Snow continued to fall without end, as I stood behind the bay window looking out at my street that had been completely blanketed by the white powder. It made Christmas day feel more like Christmas day, after having little to no snow the previous two years. Taking a final drag from my smoke, I walked over towards the fireplace, tossing the butt into the burning fire, as I looked at the framed picture of my wife Rachel, our 8-year-old twins Mindy and Mikey and myself that hung over the fireplace. Stepping away from the fireplace, I looked around the living room that was covered in Christmas decorations from top to bottom, with our Christmas tree set up in the corner of the room. All the twins' ornaments that they had made in school and at home the past two years, decorated over half of our artificial tree. Taking a final sip of Whiskey, I took a deep breath and began to follow the scent of the cooking turkey towards the kitchen. As I walked towards the stove, I looked at my watch and saw it was a quarter past two. The bird still had another hour to go. On top of that, I still needed to get the potatoes peeled and put on the burner. I dropped my empty glass into the sink, and then began to walk towards the basement door. And stopped. Standing behind the closed door, I turned the handle slowly and stood at the top of the stairs, as I heard the cage thrashing back and forth. Once I got downstairs, I looked over at the cage my twins were in, who immediately stopped moving around, focusing their dead little eyes on me. From behind them I heard a soft growl from Rachel who was tied up in a chair.

She watched me closely as I walked towards and past her, stopping in front of the cupboard that was directly behind her.

"Don't worry gang, daddy didn't forget about the mashed potatoes." I told them as I reached into the cupboard and grabbed the bag. "Bird should be ready in less than an hour," I let them know before I headed back upstairs.

Once I got to the kitchen, I stopped in front the sink and looked down at my empty glass, tempted to have another drink of Wild Turkey. Instead I opened the bag and dumped the rest of the potatoes into the sink. As I began to run the icy water, I grabbed the peeler that was on the counter, then began to think about that day Rachel and myself were watching CNN.

The reporter was in a small town in the U.S, standing in front of a cemetery, reporting on a wild story about the undead rising from their graves.

You could tell he was doing his best to take this story seriously, as he introduced a local woman who claimed she had been attacked just outside of the cemetery.

Looking at her, you could tell that something was off with said woman. Her skin was very pale, and her eyes looked all glassy.

As the reporter failed miserably not to break a smile as he begun to ask her questions. The woman suddenly grabbed him by the side of his head and bit into his neck.

Blood squirted everywhere, as the reporter screamed and was dragged down to the ground.

The cameraman made no attempt to help, as he continued to film the poor bastard as the woman tore into the reporter's gut and pulled out his intestines, beginning to feed on his rubbery innards that chewed like gristle between her teeth.

Mercifully the feed switched back to CNN control, as the news anchors sat there with looks of disbelief on their faces.

Suddenly the female anchor bent down and threw up in front of the desk.

Rachel and I sat there shocked by what we had seen.

What could have possessed this woman to commit such a horrible act?

We looked at the clock and saw it was 2:35 pm.

With the kids twenty minutes away from being dismissed, Rachel and myself decided to go pick them up.

Once we were inside the minivan, Rachel turned the radio on, and sure enough all that 620 news was talking about, was what we had just seen.

When we reached the kids classroom, I didn't bother to knock on the door, as I walked in surprising their teacher Mr. Reed.

Mr. Reed looked on as we told the kids to go out into the hall and get ready.

Mr. Reed immediately came out into the hall and asked me what was going on?

I looked at the kids, as Rachel was helping them get into their coats, then explained everything to him.

He was skeptical at what I told him. But I assured him everything I told him was very real.

As we drove away from the school, the snow began to fall. The twins wanted to go to the park and go sledding. But we told them we couldn't do that today.

Over the radio we learned more and more attacks were happening throughout the U.S. When we got home. Rachel and myself went back into the living and turned the TV back on, as the twins went to play in Mikey's room.

It was being reported now, that whoever was attacked and bitten, would soon turn into one of the undead.

The CDC had made a statement, that whatever was responsible for this, was the cause of some unknown pathogen.

The CDC had no idea how this pathogen started or where it came from. Any attempts so far that had been made to find its origin had failed.

But they warned not to encounter them. If you were bitten, you would be infected and become one of the walking dead.

Suddenly we heard Mindy coming down the hall towards us in hysterics.

"Honey, what's wrong?" Rachel asked, as Mindy stood there holding her left arm with her right hand.

"Mikey just bit me." she answered showing her mother the bite mark on her arm that had broken the skin causing it to bleed.

Rachel pulled Mindy towards her and began to sob, as I jumped up off the sofa, and began to run down the hall towards Mikey's bedroom. When I reached my sons room, I slowly opened the door and stepped inside.

There was Mikey pacing around the room. Looking closer at him I could see his skin had become pale and saw the bite mark on his right arm that had now turned a purplish dark blue and yellow. Mikey turned to look at me and stood there for a moment, as I looked back at him, my eyes swelling with tears Mikey suddenly growled, and began to charge towards me, as I narrowly made it to the door, quickly closing it behind me. On the other side of the door, Mikey growled and began to pound on the door.

"Clay?" my wife called out to me as she walked down the hall towards me.

"What is it?" I asked her.

"Mr. Reed just called me."

"What did he want?"

"He said that Mikey was bitten by one of his classmates at last recess."

"Who was it that bit him?"

"Randy."

Rachel and I had been friends with Randy's parent's Jen and Kevin for over ten years.

I remembered that Kevin had just come back from Chicago.

There was no way he could have known at the time that this pathogen was spreading through the U.S.

"Mr. Reed said after Randy had bitten Mikey, he ran out of the school yard and disappeared,"

I took my cell phone out of my front pocket and dialed Kevin's number.

The phone rang and rang until the answering machine picked up.

I didn't bother to leave a message, from what I had seen, I just expected the worst had happened.

Suddenly Mindy come charging down the hall towards me and Rachel.

Her complexion was completely different now, as her face was all pale with an unsettling look of rabid frenzy on her face.

I yelled at Rachel to get out of the way, then knocked my daughter to the ground.

I stayed away from her mouth as she tried to bite me, yelling at Rachel to open the bedroom door.

Rachel was in still shock and could not take her eyes from Mindy.

I yelled at her again, and she responded as I dragged Mindy towards the open door and tossed her inside, quickly shutting the door behind me.

Within moments Mindy had joined her brother as they both banged on the door.

Rachel looked at the door then at me, then fell to the floor and began to weep.

I stood there for a moment before I sat down on the floor next to her, taking her into my arms.

After about an hour, I was able to able to urge Rachel back to her feet.

We both looked at the door as the pounding continued, then turned away and headed towards the living room, the pounding becoming a distant sound behind us.

When we reached the living room, we sat down on the couch and cried in each other's arms until we fell asleep.

It was after nine in the evening when I awoke, and on the TV news of the outbreak had become even worse. The only latest information that they could give us, was that the only way to stop one of the undead was to shoot it in the head.

By 10:30 we learned that this had become so widespread, that 75 percent of China's population had become infected.

The Chinese government was considering nuking parts of the country that were heavily populated by the undead.

North Korea was also considering this same action,

The U.S was not prepared to consider that as an option, even though their population was now more than 60 percent infected, with many of their major cities having declared martial law.

In Canada the effects of this pathogen were spreading like wildfire.

Our nation's capital was under Martial law, as well as Vancouver, Calgary and all of Quebec and Toronto.

I flipped to a local news station that showed images of Yonge Street, that had turned into a war zone. Any police that were left, as well as any other able-bodied citizen with a gun, took up arms against the undead, that had now overwhelmed all of Yonge Street.

I turned the TV off and leaned back into the couch as Rachel looked at me, her eyes swollen and red from crying.

"What do we now?"

I looked around the living room at our Christmas tree then back at her.

"We wrap presents." I answered as I took her hand and led her away from the couch towards the bedroom.

As we approached Mikey's bedroom, we stopped outside the door and listened in for a minute.

There was an eerie silence coming from inside.

We thought better of opening the door, then proceeded to our room and got out the wrapping paper, tape and gifts, making three trips back and forth to the living room.

As we had done for previous Christmas's, I would wrap my son's gifts and Rachel would wrap Mindy's.

We wrapped the kids' gifts in under an hour, then went about wrapping our gifts to each other. After we finished wrapping our gifts, we placed them under the tree, then walked off hand in hand towards the bedroom.

I'm not sure what time it was when I awoke and realized that Rachel was not in bed with me.

I slid out of bed and walked down the hall towards Mikey's room and stopped. The door to his room was ride open and dark inside...

Where were my kids and Rachel, I asked myself as I walked down the hall and saw the door to the basement was open.

Once I reached the basement door, I saw that the light was on downstairs

Suddenly I heard a noise coming from below.

I stood there for a moment thinking of what I should do, then thought of the .38 I had locked away in my closet.

As I turned away from the open door to go get the .38, I stopped and thought to myself, could I really bring myself to shoot my own kids in the head?

Quashing that idea, I turned and then started down the stairs, stopping when I recognized the noise I was hearing.

When I reached the bottom of the stairs. I saw my two kids locked inside the dog cage, that used to belong to our German Shepard Butch, thrashing back and forth.

Once my kids knew I was there, they immediately stopped moving inside the cage and looked in my direction, as I began to walk towards them, stopping when I saw Rachel sitting directly behind them.

Rushing towards Rachel whose head was slumped down on her chest, I noticed the bite marks that were all over her arms, and underneath her neck.

On the floor next to the chair was some rope, along with a piece of paper that was underneath it.

I immediately picked up the piece of paper and saw that it was a letter that Rachel had written to me.

Dear Clay, my love

I hope by the time you find me and this letter, there will still be time for you to do what needs to be done.

I am so sorry Clay but I could not bear the fact of what Mikey and Mindy had become.

I took your gun and did what I could. it was the hardest thing I have ever had to do.

Looking at our kids, I knew all I wanted was to be close to them, even if it meant becoming one of them.

Please Clay, tie me up to this chair. Leave me to be close to my babies.

I love you so much and hope you will forgive me for what I have done. We had a great life, and I can't wait to meet you in the next.

I love you now and forever.

Rachel

I stood there trembling as I finished her letter, then looked down at my beautiful wife of 14 years. The mother of my children. The woman I fell in love with that Spring day 16 years ago when my best friend Hal had introduced us. Now she sat in front of me near death, apologising for the selfless act she had committed. An act that made me love her even more.

I swallowed hard, then began to tie her up, as I listened to her labored breathing.

Once I finished, she lifted her head up and looked at me.

Her face was now pale, as she looked at me with blank eyes, growling softly.

I stepped back from my wife, looked at my kids, then turned and headed upstairs.

When I was halfway up the stairs I heard the cage begin to thrash back and forth.

For the last week and a half, my life has consisted of small hope that they would be able to discover how this pathogen started and find a cure.

When I was not watching CNN, I was downstairs with my family

Each day when I would read and talk to them, the three of them would just sit there, listening to everything I had to say.

Two days before Christmas, CNN'S feed disappeared and every station was now broadcasting the emergency broadcast message.

I now knew any hope of a cure was not going to happen.

It was the end and I was going to celebrate one last Christmas with my family.

I checked the temperature on the turkey and saw the bird was close to being ready.

As the turkey continued to cook, I mashed the potatoes and brought them along with the rest of the food I had prepared into the kitchen.

When the turkey finally came out of the oven, it didn't surprise me that this would be the year that I would perform my best carving job.

As I brought the turkey into the dining room I looked down at the table which I had set the night before covering it with our traditional Christmas tablecloth, along with Rachel's finest China and cutlery.

Before I went to the basement, I walked back into the kitchen towards the wine rack and pulled out a bottle of Rachel's favorite Italian red wine.

Once I got to the bottom of the stairs, I looked over at my wife and kids and smiled.

The twins just stared at me, as I walked over towards Rachel whose gaze was already fixed on me.

"Easy honey. I'm just going to untie you now," I told her, keeping a close eye, as I began to undo the knots.

When I finished I expected her to attack me. But to my relief, she never did.

She just sat there staring at me, as I turned my back to her and walked over to the cage and unlocked it.

"Dinner is served," I told them as I turned and headed upstairs.

As I took my seat at the head of the table, I sat there expecting to hear frantic footsteps coming up the stairs, coming to get their Christmas feast and feed on me. But that was not the case.

After a few minutes I heard footsteps coming up the stairs, and saw Rachel appear first, as she came walking into the dining room followed by Mikey and Mindy.

Rachel sat down at the other end of the table across from me, while the kids took their seats on the opposite sides of the table across from each other, as they always did.

I sat there staring at my family wondering how long this moment would last, knowing at any second that they could suddenly turn on me.

I tapped my wine glass with my fork, lifted it into the air. then looked at Rachel first, then at the twins and smiled at them, as tears began to swell up in my eyes.

Getting to slowly to my feet, I raised the .38 and fired a single shot that struck Rachel in the forehead.

I watched Rachel come crashing down onto the table, then looked at Mikey, who had not budged from where he was sitting, and fired a single shot that hit him in the right eye, which sent him crashing face first into the table.

Turning to look at Mindy, I felt my right hand beginning to tremble. In this moment of hesitation, I expected my daughter to leap across the table at me. But instead she just sat there looking across at her brother.

I managed to settle my right hand long enough to take aim at my daughter, then fired at her, missing with the first shot as it grazed her head.

She slightly reacted to that, as I fired another shot, that found its mark in her forehead, which sent her falling to the floor with a sick thud.

With my family truly dead now, I closed my eyes, bowed my head and said grace. Suddenly I heard noises coming from outside of the house. Getting to my feet, I picked up the .38 and walked towards the living room, stopping in front of the bay window. Outside stood a large group of the undead, who were pawing at the window trying to get inside, while more and more of them converged on my house. I stood there for a moment watching them and feeling sorry for them, knowing that none of them deserved this cruel fate that had befallen them. The group outside grew larger, and the pawing quickly turned into pounding, I knew it was only a matter of time before they broke through the glass, as I watched them for another minute before, I turned and walked towards the dining room, while the pounding behind me intensified.

Slumping down into the chair, I took a long drink of wine, then dug into my dinner. Suddenly the window shattered, and I heard the undead beginning to come into the living room.

I sat there a moment, as memories of Rachel and the twins flashed before my eyes, while the undead entered the dining room and shambled their way towards me.

Fighting back the tears, I pressed the cold tip of the .38 against the side of my head and smiled.

THE SHIP

By André Cowen, Hannah Blencowe, K.A. Dutton, &
Zaynah Chowdhury

The storm came down fiercer than any conditions John had experienced at sea before and the thunderous sky did nothing to quell the uneasy feeling in his stomach. This was another trip to retrieve hauls of slack-mouthed fish, all silver and shining in their baskets for market, yet John felt different about this one. He knew his way around the boat now he had been on several haulages with the new vessel. The previous owner of the boat had passed away and his boat was sold on. Old age, it was. A cantankerous man, apparently, but John hadn't pressed further. He would be the first to admit the boat had fallen into disarray now it was in John's hands. Paint work had begun to peel away and the blood of previous haulages had stained the deck something terrible. Despite the state of the vessel, it did its job well.

He decided to take shelter in the cabin of the boat and wait out the storm. Stumbling with the force of relentless waves below the belly of the boat, John fell heavily onto the small seat and steadied himself. A chilling air had crept into the small space and, despite the bitter winds and rain outside, John sensed it was something else entirely. It sunk into his bones and clung to his teeth. Something else was here.

A boot toppled over on its side.

He leapt from his sitting place and clutched at his heart pounding manically beneath his sweater, but it did not lessen its resounding beat as a coil of rope slowly rose like a python and slivered across the floor towards him. John tried desperately to pry the soles of his feet from the floor but he was glued by a force too powerful to resist. The rope wound itself around his ankles like prisoner's shackles and the tight fibers dug deep into his skin.

John hurried to release an SOS. He prayed for a familiar voice to help him. The radio crackled into life and a distorted voice broke into the room. "Hello, is anyone there? Please respond". John clutched at the radio as the boat tipped him back and forth.

"Hello? There's something here!"

"Say again, the storm .... radio. Go back..."

The voice distorted into an indistinguishable crackle and screech. John started to shake as a figure stood on the bow of the ship in front of him, looking out into the storm in his distinguishable long coat as it blew in the heavy wind. As he turned and looked at John, a crate of fish flung itself at the window, cracking the glass in front of him. John fumbled desperately at the radio as he lost sight of the figure. The storm began to settle as the fish laid strewn on the deck and the radio signal returned.

John tried to explain, panic still induced in his mind after he pulled into the dock. The dock master approached him, concerned, as John left the boat, shaking as he walked.

"What's this about a storm? Are you alright? You said someone was with you" he asked, an edge of concern in his voice.

"That's impossible", the dock master muttered after John had explained. "There are stories of the captain searching the docks for his ship, workers have reported sightings but nothing like you've described." John looked at him as the dock master sighed deeply and gestured at the boat John had just stepped off of.

"That is his boat. He was always very protective of his boat."

A few days had passed. John was still slightly wary of being on his boat, but the fish would not take themselves to land. He had a job to do. The sea can play treacherous tricks on the mind.

Though how the rope managed to weave itself around John's ankles still escaped him. After the disaster of the storm John had noticed strange little occurrences taking place on his boat. His belongings being misplaced, problems with the gear not functioning yet he'd had the boat checked twice over and he had done it himself many times – nothing appeared to be wrong. Though the other men had remarked on the grubby nature of the hull, the boat still completed its function which was all that mattered to John. No system malfunctions, all equipment in working order, John was satisfied.

In an attempt to focus his mind, he started to raise the net from the water. A warning from the radar system startled him, a thunderstorm was approaching. John cast his eyes over the pristine waters. There was no change in the wind. The horizon looked clear. No sign of a squall on the way. Yet the imposing red alert heading quickly towards the vessel on screen caused John to grit his teeth.

Time to change course. It was getting closer. John scrambled to the radio "Mayday! Mayday! Need immediate assistance. A storm's about to hit!" The static made John's blood run cold. "Hello! Hello! Mayday!" The unchanging empty response caused his stomach to plummet to the ground. John rushed to the anchor, hoping to ride it out and pray for the best. His eyes darted around the grey sky. At any moment the choppy waves could transform into black crashing walls of destruction. The heavens would shower down rain like bullets. As the wind would whip John around like a rag doll. But the crackling of the radio sparked hope in John's fearful heart.

"Hello? Is someone there?"

"Get out. Get out. Get out." John leapt backwards in fright. The words repeated over and over again like a needle stuck on a record. John's heart was on the verge of bursting out of his chest when a man appeared in front of him. His mouth ran dry as he realised this man was floating a few inches above the deck floor. The figure stared John right in the eye.

"This is my ship." The ghost of the Captain that once was glided across the deck. Creeping towards john with a loathsome expression.

"Take it!" John pleaded, clapping his hands together in prayer. Only a miracle can save him now.

The ghost was unwavering. The waves untiring as they crashed into the boat, taking pieces with them to be lost in the endless sea. Soon, John with it.

Falling to his knees on the cold, wet, floor deck. John cried. "Please, I just want to live!"

The ghost paused. Expressionless. Then he charged. Passing through John, before evaporating into the hungry fog. He crashed to the floor to be consumed by it too.

Days later, as the fog cleared, fishermen on the docks were getting ready for the day ahead.

"There!" A fisherman exclaimed in astonishment. It was a boat. It slowly glided through the waters before docking with gentle ease. The boat that was half destroyed, in pristine condition. Not even a chip in the paint. They searched and searched the boat. But there was not a trace, nor soul, nor a body in sight.

AUTHOR BIOGRAPHIES

K.A. Dutton

Is a writer, poet, and blogger. Liminal Spaces is her first novel. She usually prefers to write in genres such as Fantasy, Fiction, and YA. Her next book will feature a collection of poetry, which will be available by June 2018. Find her on Instagram: @k.a.dutton and Facebook: @authork.a.dutton

Shannan Mitchener

Is a writer, poet, and actress. With a deep love for makeup and writing depressing poetry. She enjoys performing in plays, watching musicals, and bingeing Netflix. You can buy her debut poetry collection *Meaningless Destruction* available now on Amazon. Follow her on Instagram: @shannanxm and Twitter

@shannanalexism or search her name on Facebook to find her Author page.

Antonio Ferrara

Is a 47-year-old writer from Canada. Antonio lives with his wife and son. He has been a long-term writer with a love for science fiction, horror, and super hero fiction.

Lily Noova

Is a writer from Saint Petersburg, Russia. *The Lake* is her first completed short story in English, her second language. She is a freelance writer with a love for mysteries, curses, and fantasy. She aims to one day publish her own YA novel and picture book. You can find her on Twitter @ComradeCap.

ACKNOWLEDGEMENTS

First and foremost, thank you to all the writers that have contributed to the making of this book. Without you, this wouldn't exist, and I am so happy to have been given the chance to publish a part of you.

Thank you to my family. Especially my parents: Amanda, George, Allen, and Gemma. My siblings: Justin, Georgia, and Alicia. My Grandparents, my aunts and uncles, my cousins, and just my whole massive family. For all the support you have given me over the course of my life and on my university journey. My whole family have always supported my dream of being a writer, and I could not have done it without all of you, thank you.

Next, my friends. I have been so lucky to have always found the most amazing people and have them become such a huge part of my life. Thank you to my friend since primary school: Hannah. The great friends that I got to spend my teenage years with: Rosy, Jonathan, Ruth, and Paul, I know we don't speak as often as we used to, but I love all of you dearly. The wonderful friends that have helped me survive university: Shannan, Hannah, Sophie, Noah, Max, Judita, and many others. You are all stars. Finally, one of my best friends: Elliott. Every single one of you have supported my writing over the years, read and criticized my work, and have been my inspiration. I love you all, thank you.

To my teachers. To the one in Primary school that told me my dream to be an author would get me nowhere, you may be right but at least I'm happy. To the teachers in St Edwards Middle School and Westwood College, thank you for supporting me. To the Lectures at De Montfort University, thank you for pushing me and forcing me out of my comfort zones to become a better writer.

Thank you to the reader for buying this book, I hope you have enjoyed it.

Printed in Great Britain
by Amazon

35288281R00069